Grandfather's Lovesong

Grandfather's Lovesong

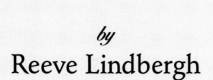

✦

by
Reeve Lindbergh

illustrated by
Rachel Isadora

Viking

I love you high
Like the top of the sky
Where the sun and moon
Go floating by

I love you low
Like the world below
Where parents watch
Their children grow

I love you wide
Like the earth's great tide
With a hug of oceans
Held inside

I love you tall
Like the autumn call
Of geese that fly
When red leaves fall

I love you bold
Like November cold
When cornfields stand
In frost and gold

I love you deep
Like winter sleep
When we curl up warm
And count our sheep

15

I love you clean
Like the pale first green
When grass appears
Where snow has been

I love you gay
Like an April day
When all young things
Come out to play

I love you fair
Like warm spring air
With earth fresh-turned
By plow and mare

I love you free

Like the wind at sea

And a white boat sailing

Home to me

I love you plain
Like summer rain
On all the round stones
On the beach in Maine

I love you clear
Like the meadow deer
Who wait and watch
When evening's near

I love you true
Like the mountain view
Where earth meets sky
And birds fly through

I love you strong
Like the sparrow's song
That sings in my heart
Your whole life long.

VIKING
Published by the Penguin Group
Penguin Books USA Inc., 375 Hudson Street, New York, New York 10014, U.S.A.
Penguin Books Ltd, 27 Wrights Lane, London W8 5TZ, England
Penguin Books Australia Ltd, Ringwood, Victoria, Australia
Penguin Books Canada Ltd, 10 Alcorn Avenue, Toronto, Ontario, Canada M4V 3B2
Penguin Books (N.Z.) Ltd, 182–190 Wairau Road, Auckland 10, New Zealand

Penguin Books Ltd, Registered Offices: Harmondsworth, Middlesex, England

First published in 1993 by Viking, a division of Penguin Books USA Inc.

10 9 8 7 6 5 4 3 2 1

Text copyright © Reeve Lindbergh, 1993
Illustrations copyright © Rachel Isadora, 1993
All rights reserved

Library of Congress Cataloging-in-Publication Data
Lindbergh, Reeve.
Grandfather's lovesong / Reeve Lindbergh;
illustrated by Rachel Isadora.   p.   cm.
Summary: A poetic description of love between a boy and his
grandfather, using metaphors of nature throughout the seasons.
ISBN 0-670-84842-5
1. Grandfathers—Juvenile poetry.   2. Children's poetry, American.
[1. Grandfathers—Poetry.   2. American poetry.]   I. Isadora, Rachel, ill.   II. Title.
PS3552.R6975G7   1993   811'.54—dc20   92-22212   CIP   AC

Printed in Hong Kong
Set in 20 pt. Schneidler Medium